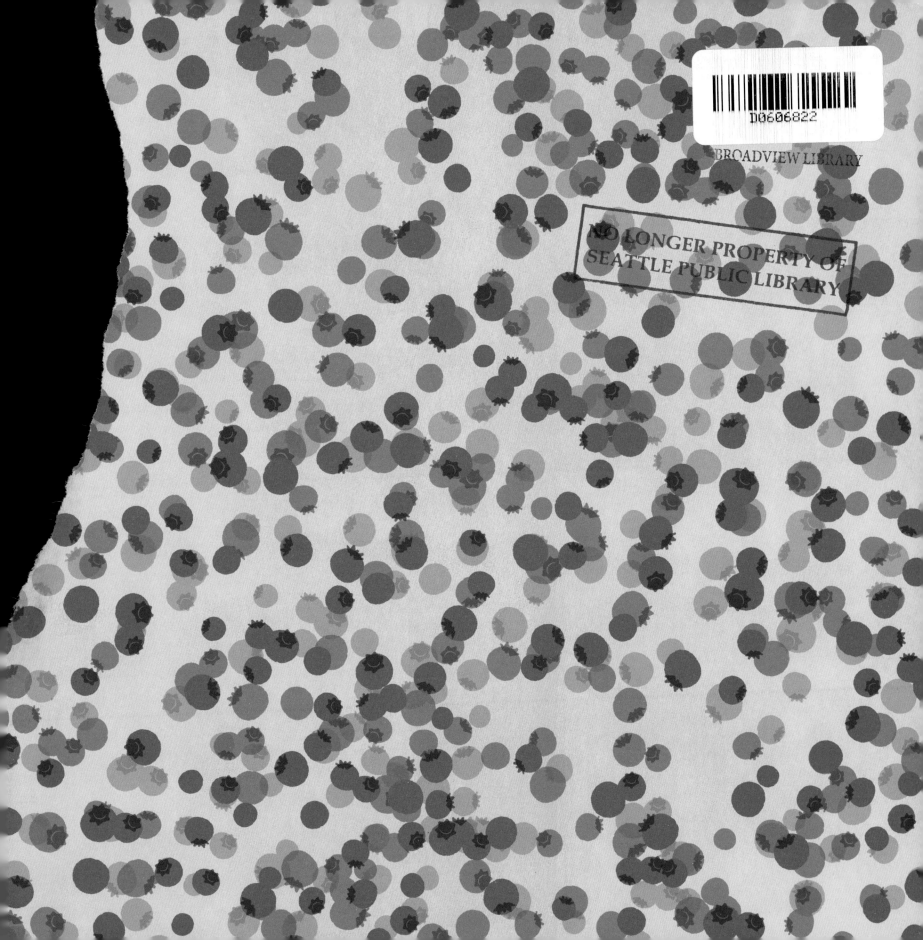

BLUE BADGER

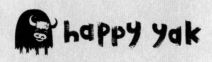

There is no reason to philosophize,
except to find happiness
—Saint Augustine

For Karl and Neil—Huw
For Julian, Ruben, and Mark—Ben

Quarto is the authority on a wide range of topics.
Quarto educates, entertains and enriches the lives of
our readers—enthusiasts and lovers of hands-on living.
www.quartoknows.com

Huw Lewis Jones has asserted his right to be identified as the author of this work.
Ben Sanders has asserted his right to be identified as the illustrator of this work.

First published in 2022 by Happy Yak, an imprint of The Quarto Group.
26391 Crown Valley Parkway, Suite 220,
Mission Viejo, CA 92691, USA
T: +1 949 380 7510
F: +1 949 380 7575
www.quartoknows.com

A CIP record for this book is available from the Library of Congress.

ISBN: 978-0-7112-6752-7

Manufactured in Guangdong, China CC112021
9 8 7 6 5 4 3 2 1

BLUE BADGER

Huw Lewis Jones & Ben Sanders

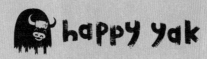
happy yak

White and black.
Day and night.
Badger doesn't feel quite right.

Who am I?

And to make matters worse...

...he now has a blue bottom.

Hello, Bird.
Am I white and black,
or black and white?

Not sure.
But can you help me untangle this?

Of course.

Thanks, Badger.

Hello, Dog.
Am I white and black,
or black and white?

I dunno.

But I like your
blue bottom.
Want to play fetch?

Sure.

Hello, Cow.
Am I white and black,
or black and white?

Why are you asking me?
You're far too small.

Oh.

Go ask Skunk.

Hello, Skunk.
Am I white and black,
or black and white?

Doesn't matter.
You're far too big.

Oh.

And you smell funny.

Hello, Zebra.
Am I white and black,
or black and white?

That's a good question.
But what about me?

Am I white with black stripes,
or black with white stripes?

Who cares?
You're not as FABULOUS as me!

Don't worry, Zebra.
Panda is always showing off.

Hello, Whale.
Am I white and black,
or black and white?

No idea.
Can you swim?

I don't think so.
I can't remember.
Do I have to?

Relax, Badger!
Go ask Penguin.

Hello, Penguin.
Am I white and black,
or black and white?

That's easy.

Really?

You're both. Just like me!

Except I can't swim...

Listen. I'm a bird that can't fly.
And I'm fine with that.
As for swimming, I bet you could if you tried.

Maybe.

And what's more, Badger,
you're kind.
And that's the best thing of all.

You can be whatever
you want to be!

Thanks, Penguin.

No worries.

But what happened to your
nice blue bottom?

Oh.
Never mind.
I'm sure it will come back.
Are you hungry?

Well, that was nice.

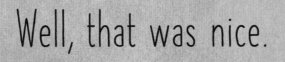